The Dog
Who Wouldn't
Be Left Behind

Canadian Cataloguing in Publication Data

Finnigan, Joan, 1925–
    The dog who wouldn't be left behind

ISBN 0-88899-057-X

I. Beinicke, Steve. II. Title.

PS8511.I58D63 1989 jC813'.54 C89-093420-7
PZ7.F566Do 1989

A Groundwood Book
Douglas and McIntyre
26 Lennox Street
Toronto, Canada M6G 1J4

Design by Michael Solomon
Printed and bound in Hong Kong
by Everbest Printing Company, Ltd.

The Dog
Who Wouldn't
Be Left Behind

Story by
Joan Finnigan

Pictures by
Steven Beinicke

A Groundwood Book
Douglas and McIntyre
Vancouver and Toronto

For Martha and Louis, Matthew the Great,
the early people at Trailhead
on Wellington Street, Ottawa,
and, of course, Clementine herself
(now age 14) — who were all
inspirations for this book.

J.F.

O NCE upon a time in the lovely capital city of Canada there lived a dog named Clementine.

Clementine was a mutsy bright. She had great blood lines. Her mother was a pure-bred border collie from Bancroft. Clementine's mother told her once that her father was, most likely, a dashing doberman pinscher on a spring junket up the Ottawa Valley. But she wasn't positive about that. There was also a handsome police dog that used to visit from Pakenham . . .

Clementine lived in the capital city with Thaddeus and Amaryllis. Thaddeus called Amaryllis Amaryllis for short. Amaryllis often called Thaddeus Taddy-love. They both called Clementine Clementine on formal and serious occasions. But they often just picked her up and hugged her and sang out,

Oh, my darling!
Oh, my darling!
Oh, my darling, Clementine.

Clementine liked living with Thaddeus and Amaryllis. She liked the food. She liked the sleeping accommodations. She liked the neighbourhood. She liked the view. And she especially liked the warm-and-snugglies galore.

Now Thaddeus and Amaryllis were owners of an outfitters called Voyageurs & Coureurs de Bois. They sold all kinds of joyous things like cross-country skis, snowshoes, canoes, kayaks, hiking boots, haversacks, jack-knives, sleeping bags and tents. They also ran a kayak school, a canoe school and out-trips all over Canada, up and down the mountains, up and down the rivers.

Naturally, their work demanded a great deal of travel. The first time they had to go away, they left Clementine with a next-door neighbour, and set off for the Sportsmen's Show in Toronto. Around about Belleville they heard a most peculiar scratching noise in the trunk of their car. So they pulled off into a service centre on the highway and opened the trunk. There was Clementine reclining on the baggage!

She enjoyed the Sportsmen's Show very much, was treated to a lot of junk food, and met a very interesting hunting hound from Hull who said he would be pleased to call on her sometime in the spring.

The next time they had to leave home,
Thaddeus and Amaryllis left the next-door
neighbour in charge. But this time they tied
Clementine to her own doghouse in her own
backyard. They also decided that she was
lonesome for her own kind. So they hired a
dogsitter, a very responsible and very large Irish
wolfhound. And they set off for Thunder Bay to
look at some new canoes that the Indians were
making there. Around about Mattawa they
happened to look in the rear-view mirror. And
what did they see there? Clementine coming
down Highway 417 dragging the Irish
wolfhound on a leash behind her.

The Irish wolfhound loved the trip up the
Agawa Canyon. But Clementine found it too
long and boring. She much preferred the
Sleeping Giant of Thunder Bay, and actually got
up one night to see it by moonlight.

Business had been going well. Thaddeus and
Amaryllis decided that they would like to take a
long holiday.

"I have always wanted to see the Seven
Wonders of the World," said Amaryllis.

"So be it," said Thaddeus, phoning the travel
agency.

Thaddeus and Amaryllis searched and scoured until they found exactly the right boarding kennel for Clementine. It had

    a. tender loving care
    b. woods to run in
    c. air-conditioning.

Then, confident that Clementine would be well taken care of, Thaddeus and Amaryllis set off to see the Seven Wonders of the World.

Thaddeus and Amaryllis were in an Air
Canada plane snoozing their way across the
Atlantic Ocean towards Egypt, Europe and the
Middle East. Suddenly the co-pilot's voice came
over the intercom. "Ladies and gentlemen.
Please do not panic. We have to report that we
have a stowaway on board. The stewardess is
going to bring the stowaway into the passenger
zone to see if any of you can identify her."

When Thaddeus and Amaryllis looked up
from their snoozing, there was the Air Canada
stewardess holding a smiling, wiggling
Clementine.

Clementine found the Pyramids of Egypt dry and unexciting. There wasn't a tree in sight, she complained. She had looked forward to seeing the Colossus of Rhodes. But when they got there, they found most of it had been destroyed by a second-century earthquake. All that was left of the Colossus of Rhodes was a toe on each side of the Aegean Sea.

But it was the Hanging Gardens of Babylon which, far and away, got Clementine's vote as the most wonderful of the Seven Wonders of the World.

By the time Clementine got home to Ottawa she had acquired a very strong taste for world travel. She had, indeed, become The Dog Who Wouldn't Be Left Behind.

So Thaddeus and Amaryllis gave up and took Clementine everywhere they went. When they went to work at Voyageurs & Coureurs de Bois, Clementine went with them and did her share. She slept in the window in the sleeping bags and in the tents and in the canoes and kayaks. Of course, everyone stopped to look at the dog sleeping in the window, and many people came into the store to meet her. Naturally, they all bought something. So Clementine became Assistant Head of Promotion.

Now, every summer, Voyageurs & Coureurs de Bois led groups of people on out-trips into the wilderness where they

a. shot the white-water rapids in their canoes

b. lived on dried food

c. slept in tents and sleeping bags for weeks

d. became one great big mosquito and black fly bite

e. had wonderful adventures

f. saw bears and wolves, owls and eagles.

Some of these out-trips ran down the "sissy" rivers like the Mississippi, and Rideau and the Jock. They were called flatwater rivers.

But other out-trips were for experts who were as good with the canoe and the paddle as the Indians who had watched over the wilderness long ago. The experts came down the Petawawa, the Dumoine and the Gatineau, and the rivers of the far north that run into Hudson's Bay and the Arctic Ocean.

Thaddeus and Amaryllis, of course, were experts. They had degrees in paddling, canoeing, out-tripping, wilderness survival, swimming and first aid. So they always led the groups coming down the wildest white-water wilderness rivers.

And, as usual, Clementine refused to be left behind.

In the land of the Midnight Sun, Clementine came down the Coppermine River and was very impressed by the caribou, the Arctic char and the Aurora Borealis.

She even went down the Nahanni, the wildest river in the world. So few humans have come safely down the Nahanni River, that they have numbers and designations. For instance, Charlie Harris of Ottawa is The Oldest Man Who Has Ever Come Down the Nahanni. He is seventy-two years old and his number is 136.

Clementine became The First Dog Who Ever
Came Down the Nahanni, and her number is
DO1. When she arrived home in Ottawa
Thaddeus and Amaryllis put her award in the
window of Voyageurs & Coureurs de Bois, along
with a fitness award that was given to her by
the Ottawa Athletic Club.

Clementine became so well known that when people signed on for out-trips, they began to ask, "Is Clementine going to be along?" If she was, the trip was usually overbooked.

Clementine was getting uppity.

Then something happened that changed the whole world. Something happened that changed everybody's world. Thaddeus and Amaryllis had a baby.

Clementine couldn't believe how much attention was lavished on this little intruder.

"How can they be so ridiculous!" she exclaimed to herself.

At first she sulked. She went around the house all day with her tail between her legs and her ears down.

She used to sleep on a corner of Thaddeus and Amaryllis's huge king-sized bed. Now she went off and slept on an old couch in the den. But nobody noticed.

Clementine became depressed. She hid under the car in the garage. She did not come when she was called for dinner. But everybody was too busy to pay any attention.

Doting aunts and uncles, grandparents and neighbours came to see the new baby. The house was filled with people ohing and ahing and oohing and ogling. But Clementine was ignored.

Clementine became angry. "That's it," she snapped. "Nobody loves me anymore. I will run away."

Clementine went on an overnight to another part of the city. She was cold and hungry. A man kicked her off his front porch. She had to sleep on the ground under a tree in a vacant lot on the wrong side of the tracks.

Back at home, Thaddeus and Amaryllis were frantic. They took turns going up and down the streets of their neighbourhood looking for Clementine, calling, "Here, Clementine," "Here, Clementine," everywhere they went.

They phoned friends and neighbours. But nobody had any news.

Finally Thaddeus said, "It is getting late. We will try again in the morning. We must get some sleep now."

"Maybe Clementine will come home in the middle of the night," Amaryllis said, close to tears.

The next morning Thaddeus phoned the city police and the dog pound. But nobody had seen Clementine. So Thaddeus and Amaryllis didn't go to work. They took turns driving slowing up and down faraway streets, calling, "Here, Clementine," "Here, Clementine."

Sometimes Amaryllis was crying as she called out, "Here, Clementine," "Oh, Clementine."

Hungry, forlorn, feeling naughty, feeling sorry, Clementine was trotting down a strange street when she heard Amaryllis calling. She put up her ears and started to run in the direction of the voice.

Suddenly she was in Amaryllis's arms, being hugged and kissed.

"Oh, Clementine!" Amaryllis said. "Don't you ever ever do that again! Don't ever run away again. Don't you know we love you?"

Safe again at home, Thaddeus scratched Clementine's ears and rubbed her back legs, just like old times.

"Silly girl," he said. "Don't you know there is always enough love to go around here?"

At suppertime Thaddeus took Clementine on her favourite walk. They went to Mr. Laflamme's corner store meat department and got her favourite beef marrow bone.

"Welcome back, Clementine," said Mr. Laflamme.

And Clementine found out that there was enough love to go around for everybody.

She became curious about the little thing. It laughed. She began to like it. Then Clementine realized that there were other things in life besides travelling around the world. "Maybe I have seen everything," she yawned.

Clementine became a guard dog. Thaddeus
and Amaryllis didn't go off on trips anymore.
They hugged the hearth and sang lullabyes.
Clementine learned a few herself.

The house was cosy. The view was lovely. There were warm-and-snugglies galore. Friends and relatives came to visit more often. The food got better and better as Amaryllis improved her cooking and watched everyone's nutrition. No more junk food.

As she groaned with pleasure beside the fire,
Clementine realized that she was ready to settle
down. Sometimes her bones creaked when she
got up too quickly. A back tooth was loose and
she had a grey hair.

She became very popular in the neighbourhood as a story teller. She told tall tales of her past adventures and all the wonders she had seen.

Thaddeus and Amaryllis liked having babies so much that they had more. And The Dog Who Wouldn't Be Left Behind became The Dog Who Liked to Stay at Home.

THE END